One Tough Turkey

A Thanksgiving Story

by Steven Kroll
illustrated by John Wallner

Holiday House / New York

Library of Congress Cataloging in Publication Data

Kroll, Steven.
One tough turkey.

SUMMARY: Recounts the "real story" of the first
Thanksgiving when the Pilgrims pursued such tough
turkeys for dinner that they had to settle for squash.
[1. Thanksgiving Day—Fiction. 2. Turkeys—Fiction]
I. Wallner, John C., ill. II. Title.
PZ7.K92250n   [E]   82-2925
ISBN 0-8234-0457-9   AACR2

for Hortense Martin, who insisted
S.K.

for the turkeys I have known
J.W.

WHEN THE PILGRIMS had lived through their first year in the New World, and it was time for the first Thanksgiving, everyone wanted turkey.

But it was hard to catch turkeys. They were all wild in the woods.

"Go and get them!" said the Governor.

"Okay," said Captain Bill Fitz, chief turkey catcher.

Captain Bill shouldered his musket. He gathered his ten best men and his son Chris. Together they set off for the woods, in pursuit of wild turkeys.

There was just one thing they hadn't counted on.

Out in the woods was one tough turkey! His name was Solomon.

As Captain Bill and his men came tramping across the field, Solomon watched them. They didn't look very friendly.

Solomon rushed back into the bushes. He put up a big
sign: NO TURKEYS! TURKEYS FLOWN SOUTH
FOR THE WINTER!

"What's this?" said Captain Bill.

"It's a big sign," said Chris.

"I know that," said Captain Bill. "What does it mean?"

"It means these turkeys are big liars. Because turkeys don't fly south."

"Then let's go get 'em!" said Captain Bill.

And he waved his musket in the direction of the woods.

Solomon ran and found his wife Regina and his two children, Lavinia and Alfred. He rushed them to the edge of the woods.

"You see those Pilgrims?" he said. "They want us for Thanksgiving dinner. We've got to stop them!"

"Right!" said Regina.

"Right!" said Lavinia and Alfred.

Quickly Lavinia and Alfred strung a rope between the trees. As Captain Bill and his men marched into the woods, they tripped and fell on their backs.

While they lay there stunned, Regina put up another sign: PILGRIMS GO HOME!

"What do you think of that?" said Captain Bill.

"They must not like us," said Chris.

"Well, I'll tell you something," said Captain Bill. "We haven't come all the way from England to be treated like this by a bunch of turkeys!"

"Yes, Father," said Chris.

"Right on!" said the ten best men.

At that moment they heard some gobbling behind a tree. Captain Bill placed a finger over his lips and gestured with his hand.

"I think we've got one," he whispered.

Everyone tiptoed toward the tree. Suddenly there was some gobbling behind a second tree, and then a third.

The Pilgrims didn't know which turkey to pursue first.

"Split up into groups, and we'll get them all," whispered Captain Bill.

But no one knew which group to join, or which group should catch what turkey. They all got so confused, they couldn't move.

Solomon had placed himself behind the first tree, Regina behind the second, and Alfred and Lavinia behind the third. With the Pilgrims so mixed up, there was plenty of time to escape.

All four of them ran to warn the other turkeys.

"Run!" shouted Solomon. "Hide in the deepest part of the woods!"

When the turkeys had fled, Solomon, Regina, Alfred, and Lavinia returned to the Pilgrims. Captain Bill and his men had regrouped in the middle of the field and were coming closer.

"I think they're in that clump of trees!" said Captain Bill, pointing.

Solomon looked at Lavinia and Alfred. "You know those bags of old feathers we've been saving to make pillows?"

Lavinia and Alfred nodded.

"I have an idea."

When Solomon had explained, the four of them gathered up the big bags of old feathers. They hoisted them up into the trees. As the Pilgrims reached the right spot, Solomon, Regina, Alfred, and Lavinia beat on the bags with sticks.

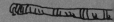

All at once, the Pilgrims were covered in old turkey feathers.

"Surprise!" the four turkeys yelled. Then they raced away into the woods.

"Do you think they'll leave us alone now?" Regina asked as they ran.

"I don't know," said Solomon. "You can't ever be sure with these Pilgrims."

Just then Chris jumped out of a tree and landed on Lavinia.

"I got you, turkey!" he shouted.

Lavinia wiggled out from under Chris and dashed into the field. Alfred ran after her.

"Look!" shouted Captain Bill. "Turkeys!"

The Pilgrims aimed their muskets. Lavinia and Alfred ducked. There was a loud BOOM, but no one was hurt.

Solomon raced out of the woods. He fluffed his feathers and charged at the Pilgrims. They hardly noticed him. They were too busy reloading their muskets.

"Father!" said Chris. "Another turkey!"

Captain Bill looked up. "Get him!" he shouted.

Solomon took off across the field. He ran around the clump of trees. He ran in and out of the woods.

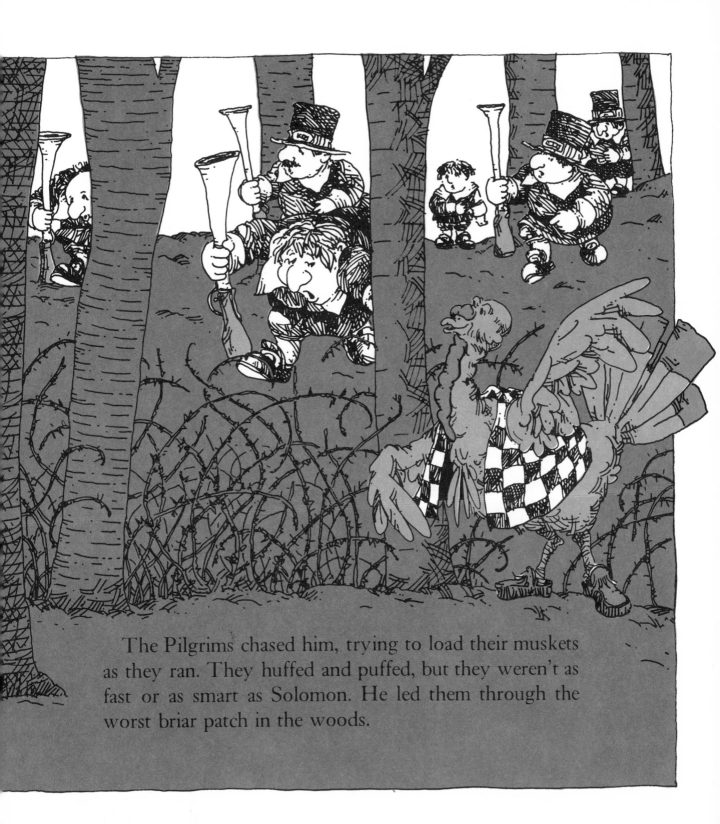

The Pilgrims chased him, trying to load their muskets as they ran. They huffed and puffed, but they weren't as fast or as smart as Solomon. He led them through the worst briar patch in the woods.

"Yowwwww!" shouted the ten best men.

"Help!" cried Chris.

"I've had enough of these turkeys!" said Captain Bill.

"We're going home!"

Solomon raced to where the other turkeys were hiding. "We fixed them!" he shouted. "Those Pilgrims won't be eating turkey this Thanksgiving!"

"Hooray!" said the turkeys. "Gobble, gobble, gobble!"

Back in Plymouth Colony, Captain Bill had to explain what had happened.

"But what about our first Thanksgiving?" said the Governor. "We've got no turkeys."

Captain Bill rubbed his brow. "Why not have squash for Thanksgiving?" he asked. "We'll just pretend we had turkey."

And that's exactly what they did. The Pilgrims ate a lot of squash at the first Thanksgiving. Everyone just thinks they ate turkey.